Dear Parent:

Congratulations! Your child is taking the first steps on an exciting journey. The destination? Independent reading!

STEP INTO READING® will help your child get there. The program offers five steps to reading success. Each step includes fun stories and colorful art. There are also Step into Reading Sticker Books, Step into Reading Math Readers, Step into Reading Write-In Readers, Step into Reading Phonics Readers, and Step into Reading Phonics First Steps! Boxed Sets—a complete literacy program with something for every child.

Learning to Read, Step by Step!

Ready to Read Preschool–Kindergarten
• big type and easy words • rhyme and rhythm • picture clues
For children who know the alphabet and are eager to begin reading.

Reading with Help Preschool–Grade 1
• basic vocabulary • short sentences • simple stories
For children who recognize familiar words and sound out new words with help.

Reading on Your Own Grades 1–3
• engaging characters • easy-to-follow plots • popular topics
For children who are ready to read on their own.

Reading Paragraphs Grades 2–3
• challenging vocabulary • short paragraphs • exciting stories
For newly independent readers who read simple sentences with confidence.

Ready for Chapters Grades 2–4
• chapters • longer paragraphs • full-color art
For children who want to take the plunge into chapter books but still like colorful pictures.

STEP INTO READING® is designed to give every child a successful reading experience. The grade levels are only guides. Children can progress through the steps at their own speed, developing confidence in their reading, no matter what their grade.

Remember, a lifetime love of reading starts with a single step!

To future readers
Brady and Francheska
—S.L. and M.L.

Text copyright © 2010 by Sally Lucas
Illustrations copyright © 2010 by Margeaux Lucas

Visit us on the Web!
www.stepintoreading.com

Educators and librarians, for a variety of teaching tools, visit us at
www.randomhouse.com/teachers

Library of Congress Cataloging-in-Publication Data
Lucas, Sally.
Dancing dinos at the beach / by Sally Lucas ; illustrated by Margeaux Lucas. — 1st ed.
     p. cm. — (Step into reading. Step 1)
Summary: The dancing dinosaurs dance out of their book and have fun cavorting on the beach.
ISBN 978-0-375-85640-2 (pbk.) — ISBN 978-0-375-95640-9 (lib. bdg.)
[1. Stories in rhyme. 2. Dinosaurs—Fiction. 3. Beaches—Fiction.] I. Lucas, Margeaux, ill.
II. Title.
PZ8.3.L966Dap 2010
[E]—dc22   2008044012

Printed in the United States of America
10 9 8 7 6 5 4 3 2 1

DANCING DINOS AT THE BEACH

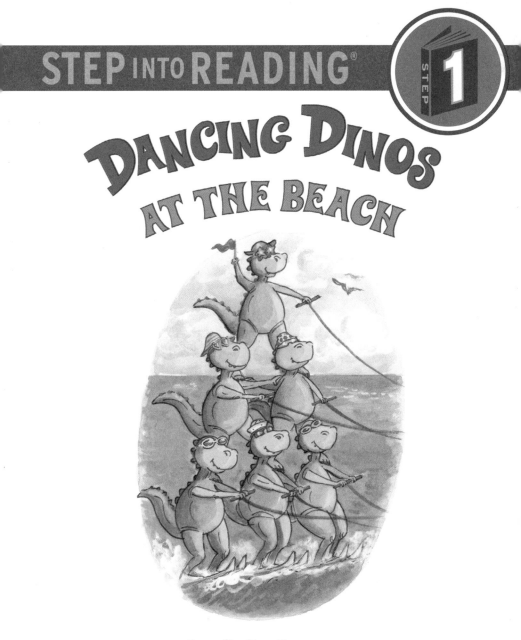

by Sally Lucas

illustrated by Margeaux Lucas

Random House New York

Dinos dancing

on page ten.

5

Dinos leaping out again!

Dinos looking
for some fun.

Dinos playing
in the sun.

Dinos digging

in the sand.

Dinos building
something grand.

Sliding, riding
round and round.

Stumbling, tumbling

to the ground.

Dinos splashing

with their tails.

Dinos filling up
their pails.

Dinos sitting

in the shade.

Dinos sipping lemonade.

Dinos feeling very brave.

Dinos riding every wave.

Dinos swimming in a V.

Dinos skiing,
one, two, three.

Dinos sailing very fast.

Dinos watching

whales go past.

Dinos tripping on a cord.

Dancing dinos—

Overboard!

Splashing, dashing
to the shore.

Bumping, jumping
more and more.

Dinos leaping in again.

Dinos dancing

on page ten.